Small Beginnings
K'Barthan Extras, Hamgeean Misfit: No 1

To Isaac,
I hope you enjoy it!

MTM xx

Small Beginnings
K'Barthan Extras,
Hamgeean Misfit: No 1

by

M T McGuire

hüp

Hamgee University Press

First published November 2019 by
Hamgee University Press

ISBN-978-1-907809-30-9

Small Beginnings is written in British English with a
couple of instances of light swearing. Estimated UK
film rating of this book : PG (Parental Guidance).

Written by M T McGuire
Edited by Emma Wilkins
Published by Hamgee University Press
Cover design by A Trouble Halved

M T McGuire is over 50 years old now but still checks inside
unfamiliar wardrobes for a gateway to Narnia.
Boringly, she's not found any.

Thank you for buying this book.
If you enjoyed it you can keep up with
news of the author online by
visiting www.hamgee.co.uk

You can also sign up for the
M T McGuire mailing list by visiting
http://www.hamgee.co.uk/freebook
and even buy K'Barthan Series merchandise at
http://bit.ly/UHSUshop

Chapter 1
A new start

The Pan of Hamgee strolled through the city, whistling nonchalantly. Actually, it wasn't exactly the city he strolled through so much as the roofs above. As a blacklisted person his very existence was treason, so walking the roofs was a bit less demanding than walking the streets in daytime. He could use the streets of course, and often did, because it was only a matter of keeping his eyes open. But sometimes he just didn't want to give it the concentration. Police patrols were thin on the ground up here. And, while he was visible from above, most of the airborne patrols were in transit. So they were either hurrying from one place to another or concentrating on some unlucky individual in the street below. Someone who was less used to being followed, usually.

There were footpads up here of course, along with a wide array of other muggers and felons. That said, as a fellow member of the criminal fraternity The Pan knew they were creatures of habit. None of them would be out until after seven and anyway, they were fellow K'Barthans. Somehow he had fewer misgivings about being murdered by a member of his own nation. So it was OK. Probably.

The Pan stopped to admire the twinkling lights of the city. It was bitingly cold but the air was fresh and clear. He breathed in deeply and exhaled a satisfyingly large cloud of steam. It felt good. He supposed it helped that he'd had a bath, visited a launderette and eaten a 'chicken' quaarl from Squeaky Joe's van. In times of hardship, The Pan considered paying for food far too much of a luxury when it could be blagged in return for odd jobs, or stolen fresh from the market every morning. He hadn't been able to afford to treat himself for several months, and the clear sinuses and pleasant chilli buzz he was experiencing were exacerbated by the cold evening air. He smiled and blew out another cloud of steamy breath, trying to make 'smoke' rings. It didn't work but The Pan didn't care. It was so long since he'd eaten a Squeaky Joe that it was like getting reacquainted with an old friend.

The Pan checked his watch. He was ahead of schedule and for a moment toyed with the idea of returning to the van for another portion. Squeaky Joe always teased The Pan about the relish with which he ate. 'You'd eat shoe leather you would!' he'd say.

'And why not? If it's cured correctly and the spices are right,' The Pan would counter. Then Squeaky Joe would give him a second tub, half price.

The Pan once asked Squeaky Joe where his nickname came from. 'Squeaky clean of course!' He'd pointed to the certificate on his van wall confirming a sky-high hygiene rating. Very possibly he'd invited The Pan to notice how spotless the work surfaces were, and how meticulously carefully all the cardinal rules of safe and hygienic food preparation were adhered to in order to allay any fears about *what* he was preparing. Because there was another rumour that the van was spotlessly, suspiciously clean because most of the meat Squeaky used was … well, put it like this, if Squeaky Joe's hot quaarl was really made with chicken he'd probably have been called Clucky Joe. But nobody ever got food poisoning or died, and since The Pan came from Hamgee, where folk were renowned for eating anything, he had few qualms about eating any substance that was prepared with as much meticulous care, and attention to hygiene, as Squeaky Joe's hot 'chicken' quaarl. That said, after ten days without food, The Pan felt his decision not to have second helpings was probably a good thing. It was rather hot for an empty stomach and was lying a little heavy.

Or maybe it was the prospect of this evening's meeting that was making The Pan's stomach feel so leaden.

Yep. Best not think about that.

He took a running jump across an alley, burping as he hit the surface of the roof on the other side, which somewhat ruined the effect of the neat landing.

'Pardon!' he said to no-one in particular. He stood for a moment, while he collected his thoughts. 'Am I really going to do this?' He felt the butterflies fluttering in his stomach, as if in answer.

When The Pan was stuck or needed to talk things through with someone, he would imagine his parents in his head, before it all went wrong, when he still got along with them. He called this 'virtual parenting'.

You're on your way to the pub aren't you? said the imaginary voice of his father.

'Not necessarily, I could blow them out.'

Blow out Big Merv? Himself? Hardly wise is it? He'll have you killed.

'Mmm, there is that.'

And you've taken his money.

The Pan's heart sank. Oh, hadn't he just? Not that much money but ... yeh. More than he could ever hope to earn and pay back.

'Very, very good point.'

That's how they get you, of course.

'Yes, I am aware.'

The Pan's gaze strayed to the cluster of bright lights in the distance that marked the position of the current phase of construction work on the Outer Ring. He didn't want to be part of a motorway flyover, not yet, although it might be preferable to anything the security forces would do to him if he was caught.

So you're going to join a gang.

'No, I'm going to run errands for Big Merv.'

Exactly, you're working for a gang lord.

'For now,' said The Pan with a sigh.

Which makes you a gang member.

'No, it makes me an employee. Gang members hang out with the boss and help him bash people.'

The Pan could think of few things he'd like to do less than hang out with Big Merv. He turned his back on the view and carried on his way. There were advantages to being part of Big Merv's organisation, he tried to tell himself as he walked. After all, he might, possibly, have just scored himself a steady income. As a Government Blacklisted Individual—a GBI—that was no mean feat. The Pan knew this was probably about as close as he'd ever get to holding down a job. Sure, he'd been recruited to work for a gang lord and yes, that was a Bad Thing. His parents, if they were still around, would definitely NOT approve. But on the other hand, he was only running errands. Small fry. He wasn't hurting anyone.

Yet. Running errands my foot. That's how it always starts, the imaginary voice of his father told him.

'Maybe,' he conceded, 'but it's not as if I'm killing anyone.'

No, just carrying the orders to kill them.

'Hopefully not. After all, I did ask him when he recruited me. And let's face it. It's not as if I can do much else, is it? In case you hadn't noticed, I'm a GBI; my existence is treason, it's illegal to employ me and if anyone murders me the security forces would see it as more of a public service than an actual crime. The only people who are going to give me paid work are people who are a bit … you know,' The Pan shrugged, 'louche about obeying the law.'

And Arnold The Prophet knew it beat starving. Or becoming one with the Outer Ring Road.

He thought about how incredible it had felt to be able to afford a portion of Squeaky Joe's hot quaarl. 'Yep, definitely.'

Chapter 2
Awkward meeting

The Pan arrived at The Parrot and Screwdriver early for his appointment with Frank and Harry. He recognised the alley running alongside it as the place where he'd spent the previous night, wrapped up warm in bin bags. At least he'd been well hidden, so with luck none of the staff had seen him. If they had, he'd probably be thrown out before he even got to meet Frank and Harry, and—

No. This was not a productive line of thought.

Despite being in an impressively rundown area, the facade of the pub was neat and tidy. The windows glinted in the feeble street lights and the frames and the door looked freshly painted. As The Pan moved a little closer he noticed that the front step had been scrubbed to within an inch of its life in a similar manner to Squeaky Joe's van. He tried the door but it was locked, which caused another fleeting moment's panic until he noticed the sign with the opening hours on. It didn't open until six. He went and found a spot out of the wind a little further down the street, wrapped his cloak around him and waited. He'd see Frank and Harry arrive from here, anyway.

By ten to six there was a group of about twenty beings waiting to go inside. Most were human but there was a Swamp Thing as well, a couple of Spiffles and a Galorsh. Soon the door was unlocked and they filed in. The Pan checked his watch. It was six o'clock and neither Frank nor Harry had shown up yet.

Arnold's pants, let this not be the wrong pub.

The Pan gave the regulars time to get pints in and get seated. Still no sign of Frank and Harry and the wind cut through his warm cloak, making him shiver with cold. No point standing about outside, freezing; he had enough cash for a beer, at least, he may as well go into the warm. As the door banged behind him the conversation petered out and all the regulars turned to stare at him. Par for the course in a place like this, The Pan supposed. Except that, clientele aside, the place was sparkling clean. Not really what The Pan would have expected when, from the looks of the area, it should have been the kind of spit-and-sawdust pub which served the dregs of society. Especially not when he took in the appearance of the other customers and realised it clearly was.

There were two staff behind the bar, a big chap with brown eyes and dark hair who looked to be in his late thirties or early forties, and a little old lady with fuzzy white hair and a wrinkled face. She came out from behind the woodwork to greet her new customer. She was small. Four foot something. The Pan was surprised she could see over the bar.

'Hello,' he said.

'Good evening,' said the little old lady, who was wearing a green, well yes, The Pan supposed it was a dress, although it had clearly seen many hard winters and boil washes. Ditto the green cardigan she sported over the top. 'I is Gladys Parker, proprietress of this establishment and that there is my son Trev.' She gestured to the bloke behind the bar. The Pan noticed how big he was as he folded his arms and nodded a greeting.

'Wotcher,' he said.

'Hi,' said The Pan.

'Is you lost?' asked the little old dear, Gladys Parker.

'Um … no. I'm meeting someone here, but they haven't arrived yet.'

Gladys Parker said something that sounded like, 'Hurrumph' and went back round behind the bar. Her legs seemed to start at the outer hem of her dress and bend bandily in to where her feet met in the middle. She was surprisingly nimble for someone of such advanced years. Or perhaps she was younger than she looked?

No.

A couple of chairs scraped back as two of the drinkers stood up. One was a fellow in a faux leather bomber jacket with curly blonde hair. His drinking companion was a big bloke with a lantern jaw who looked so double-hard he could have been made from granite. Suddenly there was an air of expectation among the other regulars.

'What does you want to drink?' asked the little old lady and then, looking at the two punters she added, 'Alan, Dave, 's alright,' before turning back to The Pan with an enquiring expression. Luckily, it seemed the two guys were not about to cause trouble, and to The Pan's intense relief, they sat down again.

'I'll have a beer please.'

The old lady started down the bar towards a pump at the far end but then appeared to change her mind and stopped. She turned and looked at him intently.

'Does you have a preference, son?'

The Pan made his way over to the bar and took his time reading the labels on the pumps. He got the impression that his choice of beer was important somehow. Although he liked beer, so it wasn't difficult to look interested. As he regarded the array of pumps, something told him that Humbert's Wallsmacker was probably the strongest beer but also, judging by the way the pump handle was just that little bit shinier and the metal label that tiny bit more sparkling than the others, that it was the flagship beverage.

'Could I have this one, please?' said The Pan, pointing to the cherished pump, 'Humbert's Wallsmacker?''

With another, 'hurrumph,' the old lady pulled him a pint of the beer he'd requested, taking care to ensure the contents of the glass settled properly before topping it up. He took a seat at the bar and pushed some of his small stack of coins across to her.

The Pan didn't know much about many things, but he could spot a good beer when he saw one. And one look at the glass of dark amber liquid placed before him told him this was definitely a good beer. OK, so Frank and Harry were on the way to meet him and that was scary, but if it all went wrong and this turned out to be his last drink, at least he was going to enjoy it. He took a sip. Yes. Definitely. He realised that there was still an atmosphere of silent expectation in the bar. Perhaps he'd better try some polite conversation.

'That is fantastic beer.'

'Thank you young man, you is clearly a con— connes— knows your onions, beer wise, if you gets me.'

'Thank you. I wouldn't go as far as to say I know my onions but I enjoy a good pint as much as the next man. Is it brewed here?'

'Yer,' she said with obvious pride.

'Well, Mrs …' what was her name? Oh yes, 'Parker. It's probably the best pint I've had in years. It's really, really good.'

She smiled and suddenly looked a lot less stern.

'I is Ms Parker, but I expects as you can call me Gladys. I doubts you've been drinking legally more than one year, my lad, but I isn't one to split hairs. I makes the beer here, with Ada, my colleague who is currently absent. Right Trev?' She turned to the large fellow standing further along the bar for confirmation.

'Right,' he said giving The Pan a nod.

'I see,' The Pan hesitated. 'I'm The Pan of Hamgee, at your service,' he said raising his glass.

He didn't notice when Trev looked up sharply, as he was too busy concentrating on Gladys. But then Trev spoke. 'I hasn't seen you round here before,' he said.

'Nope, I've been past a couple of times but this is the first time I've come inside.' He looked around him, taking in the warm glow of the fire burning in the grate, the buzz of quiet contented conversation and the punters … The Pan doubted anyone else was a GBI, but otherwise they looked as if they were all in the same income bracket as he was. 'I wish I'd come in earlier,' he said. *Because I fit right in.*

'Wipe my conkers!' shouted a voice and The Pan was forced to duck, nearly falling off his bar stool as something hurtled over his head. It was only when it landed with a squawk that The Pan realised it was a bird.

'Humbert! Humbert, come here!' trilled a female voice from another part of the building.

The bird was probably a parrot, The Pan decided, although it was impressively bald so it was hard to tell. It left its precarious perch on one of the pump handles and flew back down the bar, Gladys and Trev flapping and cursing at it as it skimmed dangerously low over people's drinks. The Pan noticed the way the drinkers held their glasses steady with one hand and put their other hand over the top and thought it wise to do the same. This meant he didn't have a spare hand to shoo the parrot away or try to discourage it, of course. Was that was why it chose to land on his shoulder? Or had it simply homed in on a new face.

'Humbert! Come here this instant!' shouted the voice. 'Leave that poor man alone.'

'Rope my futtocks!' said the parrot, loudly, pretty much down The Pan's ear.

'I'm sorry, come again?' He looked sideways at it. It didn't move. It really was very bald—he wondered how it actually got airborne. 'Hello parrot.'

'His name's Humbert,' said Gladys with a snort of disapproval.

The owner of the disembodied voice, and presumably also of the parrot, arrived. The Pan put his glass down on the bar, stood up and turned to face her, carefully, because Humbert's claws were sharp and he was holding on rather hard. The Pan's stomach lurched as he recognised her. Obviously, the whole reason he was sitting in The Parrot and Screwdriver on Turnadot Street, waiting for Frank the Knife and Smasher Harry, was because he'd accidentally picked Big Merv's pocket and the only alternative on offer was a trip to the suburbs to be concreted into one of the motorway stanchions on the new Outer Ring. However, before he picked Big Merv's pocket, The Pan had made an even more ham-fisted job of picking someone else's, a little old dear who had been dressed from head to toe in maroon chiffon. This little old dear. And now here she was with her parrot. At the least this was her local—after all, the bar staff knew the parrot's name. But The Pan suspected it might go further than that. What if she actually owned the pub? What if she was Gladys' colleague, Ada, who helped brew the beer?

Arnold's socks! Typical. Just as he'd been getting on so well.

The new arrival fixed him with a frosty glare. 'Well

11

I never,' she said, in a more acidic tone than The Pan felt necessary.

'I think this might be your parrot. Humbert, is it?' he squeaked nervously.

'No, I'm Ada Maddox,' said the old lady, being deliberately obtuse so she could take more affront.

'I'm sorry, I meant ...' The Pan held his hands out at either side of him then let them drop. Never mind, time to make the best of a bad situation. He slid off the stool and stepped away from the bar a little. The parrot on his shoulder wobbled but didn't fly away like he'd hoped. 'How-do-you-do, Ada Maddox, I am The Pan of Hamgee and I am at your service,' he said. He took off his hat with a flourish and tried to make a bow. But that was a bridge too far for the parrot which dug its claws in and hung on to his shoulder for dear life. So he opted for a quiet, 'ouch!' and an inclination of his head.

Chiffon Lady raised her eyebrows and put her hands on her hips. Smeck, she wasn't impressed.

The Pan took a panicky glance round, trying to read the situation from the way the punters were looking at him; mild interest, a dash of affront and a smidgeon of up-for-a-fight. Not one hundred per cent I want to kill you, but The Pan was prepared to bet they'd still be happy to chuck him out on her behalf. He'd have to meet Frank and Harry outside in the cold and neither Frank nor Harry would like that. They'd probably smash his face in. The Pan swallowed, then again—he couldn't be certain what being thrown out would entail, but there was a strong chance it would involve the punters smashing his face in as well.

'I'm sorry, I'd give him back but he doesn't seem to want to go.' The Pan looked sideways at the parrot next to him. It responded with a low keening noise.

'So I see,' said Chiffon Lady, tartly. Or was it? Yes, she seemed to be thawing a tiny, tiny bit. She and the other old dear behind the bar, Gladys, exchanged glances. There was a lot being said in those glances, but nothing The Pan could read. The Pan could almost feel the punters' eyes on him. No pressure then.

'I'm really, really, sorry,' he said again. He could feel himself going an even deeper shade of puce. Because both he and the old dear in chiffon were well aware that he wasn't apologising for his involuntary custody of her parrot but for nicking her wallet and then pretending to 'find' it earlier.

'Yes dear, I should imagine you are,' she said but this time her tone was a lot more kindly. Perhaps she'd forgiven him. 'Humbert doesn't usually take to strangers so you can't be all bad,' she added.

The Pan smiled and raised an eyebrow. 'That's very generous of you. As for Humbert, I'm not sure he's taken to me, exactly.'

'Oh, he wouldn't go near you if he hadn't,' she said. The Pan could feel the atmosphere beginning to relax and breathed a sigh of relief. It looked as if things were going to be OK. He risked a glance at Gladys and Trev. While Gladys' face was expressionless and a little stern, Trev grinned and gave him a thumbs up. That was a good sign.

Humbert sidled along The Pan's shoulder towards his ear and nibbled his earlobe.

'Stop that Humbert,' warned Ada.

'Arse,' said Humbert softly.

'Look, I'll go if you'd rather,' said The Pan, partly because he felt it was polite to make the offer but mainly because he was pretty sure, now, that she wouldn't say yes.

'No dear, that won't be necessary.'

Phew. Still a relief. 'I'm very glad, I wouldn't want to leave this beer.'

'Don't push it with the smooth talk son, we wasn't born yesterday,' said Gladys.

'No, I can see that. Aargh, no, I didn't mean— you're not— I mean I wouldn't imply that— Right. I'll just stop talking I think,' said The Pan.

'Good idea, lad,' said Trev with a wink.

Humbert the parrot finally decided to fly away. The Pan watched as he made a swift exit into the hall. He could just make out the flash of green-and-bald disappearing up some stairs.

Ada stationed herself behind the bar while Gladys disappeared through a door into a kitchen area behind. The Pan slipped back onto his stool and continued to enjoy his drink. He hadn't been in a pub for months. Thinking about it, he hadn't been indoors for over three weeks, unless he counted his wheels and the shelters along the side of the River Dang up on The Planes. Indeed, he began to feel so at home in The Parrot and Screwdriver that he almost forgot why he was there in the first place.

The door banged, making The Pan jump. Frank and Harry had arrived and for a second time everything stopped. Only this time, it seemed to have stopped a bit more thoroughly. Even Trev and Ada, behind the bar, ceased polishing glasses and the silence brought Gladys to the door of the room behind too.

'There you are, you little scrote,' said Frank heading towards The Pan at the bar.

Frank didn't seem to notice the silence until he was halfway across the stone-flagged floor, where he hesitated for a fraction of a second before ignoring it and ploughing on. Harry followed in his wake, apparently oblivious to the effects of his arrival. Well, they were high-profile gangsters. The Pan supposed they were probably used to it.

'Do you know these gentlemen?' asked Ada sharply. The punters looked silently from The Pan to Frank the Knife and Smasher Harry and back, trying to compute. The Pan cleared his throat.

'I—'

'Yer, we're old mates ain't we?' Harry slapped The Pan on the back. Ada gave him an enquiring look. With an apologetic shrug he turned back to his pint, Frank and Harry taking stools either side of him. The punters stared on in open-mouthed wonder.

'That's enough o' that, you lot! Your ears is flapping so hard you is causing a draught,' said Gladys. The hubbub of conversation and clinking of glasses gradually resumed.

'Frank the Knife and Smasher Harry, what an honour it is to serve you,' said Ada.

'Yer, it is.'

'I had no idea our new customer was so well connected,' said Ada with a slightly reproachful glance at The Pan. 'What can I get you?'

'I regrets that the hot dinners is not ready yet,' said Gladys, firmly.

'Such a shame but it *is* a bit early dears,' said Ada, smoothly cutting off Frank and Harry's protestations. 'You're welcome to try our famous cheese sandwiches. We also provide chutney if you want it but it can be a little fiery.'

The Pan perked up at once. Fiery chutney and cheese sandwiches? Bring it on.

'The cheese is home made,' added Ada.

'Mmmmmm,' said The Pan quietly. His stomach rumbled so loudly he had to cough to try and cover the noise. Squeaky Joe's rat in hot sauce seemed a long time ago all of a sudden.

Harry nodded.

'Give us two rounds,' said Frank.

'For you and your young friend.'

'Nah, for me an' Harry. If the staff wants fed they can buy their own.'

'For two gentlemen of your esteemed reputation, it would be on the house,' said Ada. 'Would you like a round?' Ada asked The Pan.

'Thanks, they sound delicious.'

'Two pints an' all,' added Harry, 'an' make it quick. We ain't stopping long.'

'Of course,' said Ada. 'For you, young man?' she asked The Pan.

'I'm doing fine with the one I have.'

It was strong stuff, this beer, and since The Pan hadn't had any alcohol for over a month he felt it wise to take things slowly and keep a clear head.

Harry got up and made his way to an out-of-the-way table in the corner, set a little apart from the other punters.

'C'mon you little smecker,' growled Frank, hauling The Pan off his stool by the scruff of the neck and shoving him forwards. The Pan staggered after Harry with a regretful glance at his pint, which he hadn't had time to bring with him.

Chapter 3
Mutual suspicion

In the event, the business side of The Pan's transaction with Frank and Harry was mercifully swift. They sat him down and took the seats either side of him, presumably so he couldn't run off. Then Harry fished an envelope out from his inside pocket and put it on the table, followed by a slip of paper with an address on it.

'Listen, you little smeck. You gotta take this envelope to this address tomorrow at three fifteen, get it?'

'Sure,' said The Pan.

'Then you read the script.' Frank pushed another piece of paper in front of him.

'OK.'

The Pan looked at the envelope. It was light pink and had a picture of a rabbit in the bottom left-hand corner. Weird. He read the script on the piece of paper.

'"This is from uncle Merv".' The Pan turned the piece of paper over. There was a delivery address on the other side but otherwise, that was all it said. 'Are you sure?'

'You doubtin' us?' asked Frank.

'No-no! Not at all,' said The Pan quickly.

'Don't talk to no-one, don't dillydally on the way an' don't be late. The boss don't like people who is late,' said Harry.

Frank the Knife chuckled. 'We do,' he said.

'Yer,' said Harry, 'but that's coz we gets to chuck 'em in the river.'

'Yer,' said Frank, 'we is proper partial to chucking blokes in the river.'

They're only trying to scare you, the sensible bit of The Pan's brain said. Pity it was working so well. His palms began to feel a bit sweaty and he was pretty sure he was going white.

'Nah, we're only yanking yer chain but that's what we're gonna be doing, see? If this letter ain't delivered when the boss wants.'

'It'll be there,' said The Pan.

'That's good news, mate,' said Harry with heavy irony.

'Sweet,' said Frank.

The Pan folded up the script and put it in his jacket pocket, along with the envelope.

Harry took a pull at his beer and made a face. 'Ugh, that's disgusting that is!'

Frank tried his. 'Smecking Arnold!'

'What's in this?' asked Harry.

'I tell you one thing, I'm effin' sure it ain't beer,' growled Frank.

As Frank and Harry were busy complaining about their pints, The Pan noticed Ada stepping out from behind the bar. She carried two plates of sandwiches balanced on one hand, silver-service style, and in the other she held The Pan's half finished glass of Humbert's Wallsmacker. She glided across the room, as if on air ride suspension, with only the toes of a pair of buff square-toed court shoes visible under the swathes of her maroon chiffon dress. As she put the plates of sandwiches on the table Harry rounded on her.

'D'you brew this stuff yourselves?' he asked belligerently.

'Yes,' said Ada with obvious pride.

'Then you gotta stop,' said Harry.

'Yer, whadda you put in it you daft old bat?' demanded Frank.

The Pan wished he had the courage to tell Frank and Harry to belt up. But since he didn't, he merely slid down in his seat a little and tilted his head down so his face was in shadow and the brim of his hat would hide his shame or, even better, his existence.

'That's our special pump for visitors,' said Ada.

'Tastes off to me, try it.' Ada took Harry's glass from him and sipped it. 'Oh deary me. I would be happy to replace it with another if you like.'

'It tastes like watery piss. Why would I want another pint?'

'Oh silly me, I meant would you like to try a different beer?' asked Ada. Neither Frank nor Harry seemed to notice the sarcastic tone of voice she was using, but The Pan did.

'We come to a pub where the beer tastes like bat pee and she asked us if we'd like some more?' Frank asked Harry incredulously.

'Why would we do that?' Harry replied.

Interestingly, now The Pan came to look at them, Frank and Harry's beers did have a bit of a cloudy appearance. Nothing like the chestnut brown nectar in his glass. Maybe the beer they'd been served was as horrible as they said.

'Glad this grot hole ain't on our patch!' muttered Harry.

'Boss'd close it down if it was. Effin' Nora! With beer like this I ain't hanging around!' Frank stood up.

'Ner, me neither,' agreed Harry. He nodded at Ada. 'You can keep them sarnies.'

'C'mon Harry, let's go an' get a proper drink up the club.'

'Yer.'

The two of them each took a step towards the door then, as one, stopped and turned to The Pan.

'As for you, you slimy little bleeder, you got your orders' said Frank. The Parrot and Screwdriver's regular punters watched on, open-mouthed, as he extended a pointy warning finger at The Pan, wagging it for emphasis as he spoke. 'Don't stuff up.'

'I won't,' said The Pan.

'You'd better not. You know what goes down if you do.'

Harry snickered nastily and elbowed Frank in the ribs.

'Yeh, him to the bottom of the Dang.' He strode across the floor, back to The Pan's table. The wood creaked as he put his hands on it and leaned down so the two of them were nose to nose. 'I'm lookin' forward to it.'

'You'll be disappointed,' said The Pan.

'No I won't. Not if you get sick from that crap you're drinking an' you're late …'

The Pan looked Harry in the eye. It was one of the scariest things he'd ever done. 'I'll be there,' he said with a lot more confidence than he felt.

'You'd better,' snarled Frank as Harry rejoined him at the door. Their leather trench coats creaked in unison as they turned and left. The door banged behind them and The Pan let out a sigh of relief.

Chapter 4
Smoothing things over

After Frank and Harry's departure the atmosphere in the pub lightened tangibly. The Pan of Hamgee flopped back in his seat. He took off his hat and ran his hands through his hair, made to put the hat back on, thought better of it and put it on the seat beside him. He suspected he was about to be asked to leave. The wise course would be to give Frank and Harry a minute or two to find their wheels and drive away, and then go of his own accord. But something was stopping him and it wasn't just that he wanted to finish his beer. He looked at Frank and Harry's untouched plates of sandwiches. Well, yes, there were those too, and their beers, but he was thinking of a different thing; a sense of belonging and, more to the point, of feeling welcome, that he hadn't felt since he'd first gone on the run nearly three years previously.

The encounter with Frank and Harry had caused large amounts of adrenaline to appear in The Pan's system and he felt distinctly shaky. Yeh. Time for a stiff drink. He reached across the table, picked up Harry's glass and put it to his lips.

'Oi–oi–oi!' shouted a voice from across the room.

The Pan stopped, glass still raised. Gladys was out from behind the bar and at the side of his table within seconds and again he marvelled at the speed she could move. She was definitely very spry. 'I reckons you should stick to yer own beer.'

The Pan looked up at her with a questioning expression, although not far up because even though he was sitting down and she was standing, she wasn't much taller than him. 'Sorry, I just thought that if these were on the house…?'

'They was but you doesn't want to drink them.'

'Oh.' The Pan put the glass back on the table and realised that everyone in the pub was listening when Trev called over from the bar: 'Yer, Mum's right. They'll ruin yer palette son, make the Wallsmacker taste funny.'

'Ah yes, I wouldn't want to do that,' said The Pan. 'Why don't I drink them after the Wallsmacker?'

Gladys sniffed. 'I suggests you doesn't,' she said.

'Yer,' agreed Trev.

'Any particular reason?' asked The Pan, picking one glass up again and holding it to the light.

'I see you does not know about running a pub,' said Gladys.

'No. You have me there.' The Pan flashed her what he hoped was a charming smile. It had no discernible effect on her expression. 'But it's only beer. What's the problem?'

'Only beer! Gracious young man, I can see we will have to educate you.' Ada had appeared behind Gladys, as if by magic.

'Yer, beer is made with yeast, see? An' yeast is a living org— org— thing. It ain't never, "just beer" cos with the yeast what's been in it, 's alive.'

'I see. Should I apologise before I drink this then?' he asked, holding Frank's glass aloft.

'Put that down, you daft lad. Like I says, I can see you hasn't no clue.'

'Exactly,' Ada chimed in. 'Let me explain. You see, dear, it's like this. Imagine you've left work and come to the pub to relax. What's the last thing you want to see?'

'Um … two gangsters?'

'Well yes, in theory, unless you are a gangster, but I meant—'

The fellow with the curly blonde hair and the black faux leather bomber jacket piped up from a nearby table. 'Your boss!'

'Yes, of course, silly me. Sorry, I'm ...' The Pan stopped. He was about to tell them that he hadn't got a job but he realised, with a sinking feeling, that that was no longer true. Then again, thinking about his boss: 'I can imagine it would be less than relaxing.'

'Exactly,' said Ada. The guy and his drinking companion, the big bloke, nodded sagely in assent.

'Yer,' said Gladys.

'Right,' said The Pan.

'What Alan there is saying, see, is that we entertains the dregs of society in this pub.' She gave The Pan a bit of a look. 'I reckons you'll fit in nicely.'

'But your friends won't,' explained Ada cheerfully. 'It's all about market dynamics.'

'It is?'

'Yes. This is a certain kind of area and those who live here are a certain kind of being.'

'So, let me get this straight,' The Pan scratched his head, 'you're saying you serve crap beer to people you don't like so they won't drink in your pub?'

'I think that's a slightly undiplomatic way to put it, dear,' said Ada.

'But it's what you mean isn't it?'

'Yer,' agreed Gladys, 'but we calls it something different.'

'Our sales vortex,' said Ada.

Even The Pan knew that was wrong. 'Isn't it a sales funnel?' he asked.

'Ner. It's a vortex on account of the ones we likes gets

sucked in and the ones who is unsuitable gets thrown out of the side.'

'What? By Trev over there?'

'No dear, it's just a figure of speech. We are simply filtering out the customers who are unsuited to our product.'

'By giving people like Frank and Harry crap beer, so they won't come again, because your punters all work for them?' asked The Pan looking round him.

'To be completely accurate, dear, while our punters may well work for them, it's more the ones who are working for people *like* them we are worried about. Then there are the ones working independently in a way that might make people like Frank and Harry regard them as competition and come to look for them. We don't want them being found here.'

Despite their rather disparaging summation of their customer base, and him, as 'the dregs of society', The Pan felt strangely flattered to have been served a decent pint. 'Is this an invitation to come here again then?' he asked, gesturing to his beer.

Ada and Gladys exchanged glances and then Gladys folded her arms and said, 'Yer.'

'You mean ... soon?'

'Yer.'

'I'm honoured.'

'Yer. You is.'

The Pan was amazed. He was a man who was continually on the run, and not just from the authorities. Now, it appeared that in the middle of all that hiding, conniving, cheating and fleeing, he had a chance of something as normal, as homely as a 'local' pub to go to. 'What about Grongles?' he asked. 'You can't discourage them with beer—they don't drink.'

'Nah, but they only comes to places like this because

they is conducting a search,' Gladys explained.

'Yes,' Ada agreed.

'And we has contacts,' Gladys put one finger on the side of her nose. 'We knows when they is coming.'

'We can't have our customers getting arrested, we'd go bankrupt in no time!' said Ada.

'Yer,' called Trev from the bar, 'there wouldn't be none left! Too many of 'em are arrestable.'

'Too right,' said Alan from the next table. 'Half of us are supposed to be helping the police with their enquiries, right Dave?'

'Don't look at me,' grumbled the granite-jawed bloke sitting next to him.

In the background, The Pan could hear the other customers chuckling quietly into their pints and he bowed his head to hide his smile. When he looked up again, making eye contact with Ada, she wasn't expecting it. People never were when he did that. It clearly caught her by surprise. 'Were you some kind of marketing guru in a former life? Only that's genius,' he said.

Ada went a bit pink and turned to her friend, Gladys as if for moral support. 'Thank you. And never you mind what I did before, young man.'

'I was wondering, have you two taken any ...' How to put it? '... customer-discouragement measures with these sandwiches?' asked The Pan.

'What's it to you, young man?'

'Well, I was going to offer to eat them, you know, as a public service.' The Pan was pleased when the old ladies laughed.

'Cheek of it! We has a rum 'un here an' no mistake,' said Gladys, directing her comment to the whole room. Some of the punters laughed too.

'Did you adulterate the sandwiches Gladys, dear?'

asked Ada with an almost coquettish wink at The Pan.

Gladys sucked the air through her teeth like a builder about to quote for the longest and most expensive job in history. 'Ner, not so's you'd notice. I has added extra chutney.'

The Pan raised an eyebrow at her and pulled Harry's plate towards him. When he went to open one of the sandwiches, to see what the filling comprised, the bread was soft and slightly warm, while the crusts had the brittle flakiness of a newly baked loaf. It was brown bread with seeds in, which had surprised him initially. But now, in light of what Gladys and Ada had said about discouraging the wrong customers, he could imagine it was just a bid to deter Frank and Harry, whom he suspected were sliced white and pie men, straight down the line.

'The bread looks as good as the beer. Is that home made too?'

'Yer, we makes it ourselves,' said Gladys. 'And we makes the cheese. I makes the chutney an' all. I warns you, 's hot mind.'

'No problem, I'm from Hamgee. You know what they say about us.'

'That you're all reprobates?' asked Ada. The Pan suspected she was talking about his attempt at scamming her in the market, but this time her tone was light-hearted joshing rather than stern.

'I think you know the answer to that one, after this morning,' he replied in kind. 'I meant that we Hamgeeans like spicy food, so I'm sure I'll like hot chutney.'

'Maybe not this hot, dear,' said Ada as The Pan picked up a sandwich and bit into it.

The cheese was delicious, nutty yet strong, the butter and chutney melting into the warm bread. It was heaven.

Very, very hot but heaven nonetheless. He could see why the old ladies had warned him.

'Mmm,' he said and hurriedly swallowed the first mouthful. 'I imagine that would have filtered Frank and Harry out. They don't strike me as the kinds of people who'd appreciate heat levels like this.'

'Does you want me to take them sarnies away?' asked Gladys reaching out for Frank's plate.

'No! Thank you,' said The Pan, pulling it towards him and arranging it next to Harry's. 'I'll tidy these up … unless any of the other punters want some, or Trev over there?'

'You want some, son, anyone?' called Gladys.

'Nah, I'm good,' said Trev and a murmur of noes rose from the punters.

'Looks like they is all yours,' said Gladys.

'Don't blame us if you get heartburn,' said Ada.

Heartburn! Ha! That's the least of my worries, thought The Pan as he felt the unfamiliar shape of the envelope in his jacket pocket.

Chapter 5
Trouble brewing

Not far away, across the river in Big Merv's night club, Frank and Harry were talking about The Pan of Hamgee.

'I reckon the boss 'as lost his marbles on that one,' said Frank.

'Yeh, a little scrote like that ain't never gonna toe the line.'

'He's a right clever clogs an' all,' said Frank.

'Yeh. Big risk,' Harry agreed.

They sat in silence for a while, enjoying their fizzy lager and portion of chips each. It being a nightclub, these were the most expensive chips in Ning Dang Po, but since it was Big Merv's nightclub Frank and Harry got their chips for free. There was something supremely satisfying about that.

'Yeh. I dunno about you but he makes me nervous. I got a lot invested in this organisation and I reckon that little Hamgeean nerk is the kind of bird who'll sing. The security forces get one whiff of him an' we're all in trouble,' said Frank

'You're tellin' me Frank. An' I said as much to the boss.'

'Yer me an' all. An' you know what the boss said? He said he reckons the security forces ain't gonna be touching The Pan of Hamgee,' grumbled Frank.

They shook their heads in mutual resignation.

'How the smeck does he reckon that, then?' asked Harry.

'He said, they ain't gonna catch the little Hamgeean

nerk cause we couldn't,' said Frank morosely.

'We did though.'

'Nah, not really Harry. He walked into us when he was off guard.'

'Same thing innit? We still got 'im.'

Frank shrugged.

'Maybe but the boss reckons not. On account of that it's cause the little scrote got dumb rather than cause we got clever.'

'I don't like to go against the boss,' said Frank.

'Nah, me neither but it had to be said.'

'Talkin' about Big Merv, you know he's shagging that exotic dancer, Ms Myrtle?'

'What the one with the big …?' Harry put his cupped hands in front of his chest and jiggled them up and down.

'Yer, her. I reckon she's turned him soft.'

'Don't matter. It won't last, never does.'

'Nah. But right now I say he's gone too easy on that little Hamgeean smeck. So I reckon we should take steps. If you get me.'

'He'll kill us.'

'Nah, he'll thank us I reckon. Specially if we make it look like an accident.'

'I wouldn't be so sure about that.'

'I would. See, I found this.' Frank took a folded piece of paper out of his pocket and spread it out on the table. It was a wanted poster, featuring a familiar figure but without the hat and cloak.

Harry sucked air through his teeth. 'Blimey. Wanted dead or alive.' His eyes met Frank's. 'Effin' Norah! That's a blummin' big reward. Have you shown the boss this?'

'Nah. I only found it a couple of minutes ago, it was on the ground outside. You wanna take more notice of what's going on around you mate.'

'Cut the crap Frank, we ain't got time for a lecture. We gotta show that to Big Merv, now, pronto like.'

'He's off somewhere with Ms Myrtle.'

'Then we gotta phone 'im.'

'If you remember, he gave us strict orders that he didn't want no blummin' gits like us disturbing him with business until tomorrow morning.'

'Oh.'

'Yer, "oh". Listen Harry, I reckon this is something we gotta deal with on our own.'

'He might be a four-star plonker, The Pan, but you can't grass him up. It ain't honourable. And Big Merv would never let us, not even for that kind of cash.'

'Nah, *I* can't grass him up ...' Frank left the phrase hanging.

'I'm not smecking doin' it.'

'No-one said you has to.'

'Same goes for slotting 'im an' all without the boss's say so.'

'I told you, you ain't gonna have to. I just saw Fists McDermot an' he's gonna do it.'

'What, slot 'im?'

'Nah, more like, grab the package an' do the delivery, instead.'

'OK, first, how's Fists gonna find 'im, and second, how's he gonna get it off 'im? He's blummin' fast.'

'We know where the drop is, don't we? An' there's a phone box at the bottom of the street—'

'A phone box?'

'Yer, an' then 'e—'

'What? In The Planes?'

'Yer in The Planes!'

'Ain't The Planes too posh?'

'Nowhere's too posh for a phone box.'

'Get away, I don't believe yer.'

'Will you shut up about the smeckin' phone box, you toe rag, and listen? Fists is gonna go up The Planes, wait in that phone box, an' when The Pan of Hamgee walks past, he's gonna ring in a sighting.'

'What if he gets to the drop an' they hide him?'

'No-one'll hide that little git. Anyway, he won't even make the delivery. The Grongles'll be up there and on him like a ton of bricks before he even gets to the house.'

'That's it?'

'That's it.' Frank stuffed the last of his chips into his mouth. 'You wanna come down the gym and work this off tomorrow morning? Give ourselves a nice tight alibi, an' that little Hamgeean turd'll be out of the picture by the time we're done. Win-win, I reckon.'

Chapter 6
Disastrous delivery

T he Pan always felt a strange disconnect with reality in The Planes. For starters, the beings living there were all rich and, that being the case, many of them were Grongles. But for a K'Barthan to be rich enough to own or rent property up there they had to be even more well off than their Grongle neighbours—in real terms anyway—because of the exchange rate; one Grongolian dollar was worth thousands of K'Barthan zloty. And while the real estate was all sold in dollars, it was illegal for K'Barthans to own them so they had to pay in zloty at an even more unfavourable rate of exchange than usual.

Even so, it appeared Big Merv's contact had managed it.

The Pan liked The Planes and spent a fair bit of time there. When a man's existence is treason he has to be careful walking about in daylight hours. On the other hand, it's amazing how much walking about a man whose existence is treason *can* do, unmolested, if he goes to the right places. The Planes was the kind of area where people were far too well off to care about the kind of reward The Pan commanded. As long as they didn't feel that their property or safety was threatened, they were unlikely to cast a second glance at any pedestrians on their streets. They'd assume they were just staff working for their neighbours. Provided The Pan looked reasonably tidy and presentable, and he ensured that he did, it was perfectly possible for him to visit the more well-heeled areas of the city unmolested if he spaced his visits out enough.

Conversely, in poorer areas, where beings were on the lookout for blacklisted folks as a way to earn, The Pan would always take to the roofs, trees, garden walls, anywhere people wouldn't be looking for … well … other beings. He doubted the genteel inhabitants of this area ever joined the throng of folks reading the poster sites at the street corners and squares, squirreling away the facial features of any potential meal tickets they could report on sight. Then again, their staff might.

Usually The Pan would simply have driven but his temperamental wheels were currently being repaired. Since Big Merv's cash advance had covered the cost he'd dropped his snurd SE2 off at the garage and into the capable hands of Gerry the Work Experience Creature, paying for the work in advance without a second thought.

Having decided that he'd walk the streets of The Planes as if he had every right to be there, The Pan was surprised how hard he had to work to hide his expression of amazement at the houses in Tallidor Road. Even for The Planes they were amazing.

'Very smart,' he muttered. He was early and since this was an extremely salubrious area and The Pan, for all his efforts to look neatly presented, was not salubrious, he decided it was best to keep moving and keep up the appearance that he was on his way to somewhere. Someone walking in this area was one thing, but someone loitering was an invitation for the locals to mistake them for a burglar and call the police. He was supposed to deliver the envelope to number fifty three so he decided he would do a dry run first; walk past the drop point and identify exactly which house it was. It would definitely be a bad idea to knock on the wrong door.

At the bottom of the street he passed a phone box. He thought about ducking inside and pretending to be making a call for a few minutes while he checked his surroundings but someone was already there; a huge bloke with a smashed-in nose had the handset pressed to his ear. Even in this freezing weather he wasn't wearing a coat, or even a jumper—just a tight red t-shirt which showed off his intimidating array of muscles. He was a big bloke; an enforcer, for sure. One of Big Merv's, checking on The Pan's progress? Possibly. Or maybe not. The 'business' people around here probably had enforcers of their own.

The large bloke didn't appear to notice The Pan, which was strange. No enforcer worth their salt would fail to show some awareness of the presence of another being. So either he wasn't an thug or— no, he was definitely a professional thug and his lack of awareness was deliberate. He knew another being had passed him and that made The Pan wonder, with a sinking feeling, if this fellow was on the phone reporting his presence. He began to experience a strong sensation that all was not well. Even though this was a residential street, and even though this was The Planes, walking into an ambush felt the same wherever he was. He'd never ignored his instincts before and he wasn't about to start now. Ten or twenty yards on from the phone box, he stopped. 'Right,' he muttered, 'what next?'

He still had to work out which house number fifty three was. Maybe just deliver and have done. It was probably better to arrive early than not at all.

After nearly three years on the blacklist, The Pan's evasive skills were second to none. He had his own personal reason for this, a secret he divulged to no-one. He had eyes in the back of his head. They hadn't always been there—they'd grown, overnight, four years previously, when he was sixteen. The extra eyes had appeared shortly after the Grongles beheaded the Architrave, K'Barth's spiritual and temporal ruler. That particular Architrave was probably the most useless ruler in history, little more than a puppet. Even so, he'd been ordained by Arnold the Holy Prophet and chosen by the priests. So putting him to death was a special kind of sacrilege. Not that anyone did anything. It should have started a revolution but all the other K'Barthan leaders had already been executed, so no-one batted an eyelid.

As far as The Pan was concerned, suddenly growing an extra pair of eyes had merely been the culmination of a grim two weeks. At the time, he'd assumed it was all part of growing up and being Hamgeean. He'd meant to ask his parents about it, but before he'd screwed up the courage, the Grongles had carted them away. Being able to see in two directions at once had given him vertigo to start with but now he didn't give it a second thought. No-one seemed to notice the eyes under his hair, and the shadow cast by the wide brim of the hat he wore also helped to conceal them. With all that hair in front of them, The Pan had no idea how he could see anything through his extra eyes, but they obviously weren't quite the same as normal eyes because, somehow, he could.

As he stood and took the paper Frank and Harry had given him from his pocket, re-reading the delivery address, he watched the enforcer in the phone box behind him. Thinking it was now safe to do so unobserved, the guy was looking straight at The Pan.

Hmm. Not good, The Pan thought and walked on up the street, checking the house numbers, scanning the road behind him as well as in front. Then he heard it. In the distance but coming closer. Sirens.

So my broken-nosed friend, you were dobbing me in, were you? Yes. Clearly. 'Git!' muttered The Pan.

Right then, only one thing for it, deliver the letter and scarper. It was too late to hide or head up to the trees and roofs—not that he'd get far. Here the houses were so far apart that even The Pan would balk at making the leap from one to the next—nope, he had to find the drop site quickly and get indoors. If they were the right kind of contact they might be understanding if he asked to leave through a back gate or over their garden wall. He wished with all his heart that his wheels weren't at the garage being repaired. Escaping in a vehicle was always easier than on foot.

He began to jog up the street. Not so fast as to arouse suspicion or so he'd miss the house he was looking for, but not so slow that the approaching sirens would get there in time to intercept him. He could feel his pulse rate rising and sweat prickling at his hairline. It seemed to take forever as he checked the numbers on the long drives. Finally, he found the place. It was a large white stuccoed mansion with a turning circle in front and wrought-iron security gates. The sirens were getting closer. The Pan pressed the button on the entry phone and waited. Nobody was answering. He checked his watch. He was five minutes early.

A couple of hundred yards away the enforcer stepped out of the phone box and started walking towards him.

'Smeck.' The Pan pressed the button again and cast his eyes to heaven. 'Come on …'

After what felt like an eternity it was answered. 'Hello,' said a sultry female voice.

At last. 'Hi,' said The Pan. Now, what was he supposed to say, oh yes, that was it: 'I have a message from Uncle Merv,' that was as near as dammit. 'D'you want me to post it through the letter box?'

'No, come in.'

There was a buzz and The Pan pulled at the gate, hard. Nothing. 'Smecking smeck!' The enforcer was running now. 'Arnold's bottom!'

'Push the gate firmly, it sometimes sticks,' said the sultry entry-phone voice, at the edges of The Pan's consciousness, almost drowned out by the screaming of his panic-stricken thoughts.

He shoulder-charged the gate, aware of the pain as he misjudged it and made contact with an unnecessary amount of force but still, no point taking any chances as he didn't have time for it to stick. The enforcer was yards away as the gate opened and The Pan tumbled through it, pushing it closed behind him. The buzzing stopped and the gate locked with a click. As he turned and ran towards the house The Pan heard it clang under the impact of Mr Broken-nose as he had a go at getting through anyway. He put his snarling face to the railings and shouted something The Pan couldn't make out. But judging by the way he was shaking his fist it was derogatory.

The Pan turned round, made a bow and blew him a kiss.

You really are an idiot, said the sensible part of his brain.

'Yeh,' said The Pan quietly to himself as he bounded up the steps. At the top he stopped in front of the shiny black front door, rubbing his shoulder.

Somewhere, next door presumably, he could hear shouts and screams that suggested a children's party was going on. As he reached up for the knocker, the door was opened by a female Swamp Thing. She wore a smart, figure-hugging dress on the kind of body that would make a supermodel jealous. A wall of screaming-children noise hit The Pan. OK, so the party was here.

The Swamp Thing lady was every bit what her dulcet tones down the entry phone suggested; tall, statuesque with high cheekbones and a captivating grace of movement. The Pan tried not to ogle but feared he was failing dismally. Then she smiled and it lit up her face. It was all he could do to stop himself from actually saying 'wow' out loud. Could she be a girlfriend of Big Merv's? The Pan supposed it wasn't beyond possibility but she seemed out of even the boss's league. Upon reflection, she seemed out of anyone's league. She had genuine beauty. It wasn't just her face that lit up when she smiled, something in her eyes did too, as if all the goodness in her soul was shining out of them. As she smiled down at him he noticed her antennae were moving backwards and forwards, a sure sign of thought in a Swamp Thing.

'Hello there,' she said, 'you're a teensy bit early.'

'I know, I'm really sorry,' The Pan spread his hands out on either side of him, in a typically Hamgeean gesture of resignation. 'I didn't want to wait on the street, you know, it looks a bit odd, a humble messenger like me loitering outside a place like this.'

'Uh huh. That's OK. I'm sorry I took so long to answer you but I was on the phone. Would you like me to buzz the other gentleman in?' she asked.

'Who?'

'The guy who was with you?'

'With me? I came here alone.' The Pan tried to appear nonchalant and failed. She nodded with an expression The Pan couldn't quite read.

'The guy out there, he's been in the phone box for a while. He wasn't waiting for you then?'

'Not as far as I know.'

She gave him a long look, her expression completely unreadable, but all she said was 'OK.'

Her eyes were dark brown, The Pan noticed, which was unusual in a Swamp Thing, since their eyes were usually green, felt-tip green and piercing, like Big Merv's. The Pan tried to flash her a confident smile but he could see she had him bang to rights.

'Come on in then,' she said standing back and opening the door wider.

'Should I take my boots off?' he asked as he entered the hall.

She smiled again—blimey, she was stunning. No, no, no. This was no time to be distracted. 'Don't worry. It'll give the cleaners something to do.'

'Is that fair?'

'In this case yes, they're Blurpons and they keep telling me off for not making enough mess. So,' she continued as she escorted him across the hall, 'was he following you?'

The Pan gave her a bit of a look. 'I couldn't say.'

'No. I guess not, you people are a very secretive bunch,' she added, taking The Pan's noncommittal words exactly as he'd meant them. 'Don't worry, Big Merv and I are good friends, I know what he does.'

'You do?'

'Of course. How d'you like working for him?'

Arnold's socks! She was direct. 'I'm quite new to it.'

'Wait here,' she showed him into a luxurious sitting room and disappeared.

The Pan took off his hat and cloak, walked carefully across the cream carpet and sat down gingerly on one of the pristine white leather sofas. He made sure he chose one well back from the window. He put his folded cloak on the floor beside him with his hat on top.

Outside in the street, beyond the high railings and electronic gates, the security forces arrived. An armoured carrier screeched to a halt, followed by a prison van. Both switched off their sirens uncharacteristically fast. Presumably they didn't want to disturb the residents. The squashed-nose gentleman who'd been following The Pan was still at the gate and the Grongles in the vehicle leapt out and surrounded him.

The Pan saw him shake the hand of the Grongle in charge and point to the house.

'Arnold's toe jam!'

He felt his pulse rate rising and the cold sweat beginning to prickle at his temples. Would they come here? They would surely. Maybe there was a back entrance. He'd ask the Swamp Thing lady. He grabbed his cloak and hat and stood up. He couldn't tell what was being said out there but there was no harm in being ready to run.

However, from what he could glean, watching from the window, things were going wrong for the enforcer. The Pan watched as his arms waved and his head nodded as he remonstrated with the Grongle. Then the Grongle pointed at the house.

Two other Grongles stepped up and took each of the enforcer's arms. He was still talking nineteen to the dozen and struggling against the grip of his captors as they began to manhandle him towards the prison van.

The Pan ran to the window.

'No!' he shouted, because no-one deserved that, not even a man who thought *he* did. Even over the sound of the children screaming and giggling in the room next door, he could hear shouts outside as the fellow pleaded desperately and to no avail. Then for a moment his face turned towards the house and his petrified gaze met The Pan's before the Grongles dragged him into the prison van, despite his protestations. The metal doors clanged shut and it drove away.

'Smeck! What have I done?' said The Pan.

'Got here just in time, I'd say.' The lady of the house was back. She was wearing a dark wig, with her antennae tucked under it, and sunglasses.

'We can't let them take him. It's— it's not the K'Barthan way.'

'He was happy enough for them to take you.'

'Yes but, d'you know what they do to people like him?'

'Yes I do. Nothing.'

'No, it's very much something.'

'No. He'll be out with a caution for wasting police time and he, or the people who encouraged him to do what he did, will never question Big Merv's decisions about who he chooses to employ or what they do ever again.'

'Arnold's trousers, that's ...' The Pan began but words failed him.

'Business,' she smiled. 'It's simple economics. He gets stuck inside for a week or two, well, that's very inconvenient for him and his employers. But they have lawyers and contacts so he gets out and they get their valuable, highly-trained employee back. You go and Big Merv loses a skilled employee forever.'

By The Prophet's nostril hair, she was ruthless. 'I'm not skilled.'

'Big Merv must think you are. Or perhaps you have something that can't be taught.'

'You think? Feel free to clue me in.'

'You'll understand one day, when you're a little more confident.'

The Pan raised an ironic eyebrow at her. 'Thanks,' he said.

'You know, I think your tail might have been one of Merv's men. I'm sure I saw him at the club the other evening,' she said.

'And you still dobbed him in?'

'Of course. If he is part of our organisation, I have total confidence we can get him out of gaol. Although, if he's one of Big Merv's employees and he's gone against the boss's wishes, he might prefer to stay there.'

The armoured personnel carrier was still parked on the street, and as The Pan watched, the Grongle officer in charge of it walked towards the gates of the house.

'Don't move, sweetie, this is nothing to worry about. I'll be right back,' she said, as the entry phone beside the front door buzzed. The Pan realised that, to the unsuspecting policeman, she would easily pass for a Grongle if she spoke their language well enough. Presumably she did. Better not ruin all her hard work by getting himself recognised. He backed away from the window so he couldn't be seen from the road and watched his hostess walk towards the gate. She didn't open it but spoke to the officer through the bars. He didn't seem to mind.

The Pan realised that the noises of the party had abated somewhat and a small Swamp Thing child had slipped into the room. She must have been about ten, The Pan thought, but already showing the first signs of her mother's poise and good looks.

'You got my card then, Mister?' she said.

So *that's* what it was. He pulled the envelope out of his jacket pocket and turned to face her. 'Are you Jacinda Myrtle?' he asked, keeping watch on events going on at the gate with the useful extra set of eyes in the back of his head.

'Yep, but everyone calls me Jackie.'

'This is from Uncle Merv,' said The Pan, as directed in his script, 'Blimey! And I thought that was a code,' he added.

The little one laughed and took it from him with a curtesy. 'Thank you.'

Very polite. 'A pleasure,' said The Pan and bowed. He watched while Jackie opened the envelope.

'Oh.' She sounded a little disappointed. 'It's a book token.'

'Is that so bad?' asked The Pan.

She shrugged. 'Depends. Uncle Merv wants me to go to school and get an education so he gives me book tokens. It's OK, I like reading usually, but I like stories and Mum always makes me spend them on text books.'

'You don't like school then?'

'No. There's no point. I want to be a dancer like Mum.'

In spite of his heightened state of fear, or perhaps, because of it, The Pan laughed. 'I used to hate school too. Thing is, though, now that I can't go anymore I'd give anything for a second shot at it.'

She put her head on one side and looked at him thoughtfully. 'Really? Why?'

'The stuff I know has been pretty handy. But if I'd paid attention I'd know a lot more stuff, which would be a lot more handy. Who knows, if I was still there, I might have turned out smart enough to do something worthwhile with my life.' Arnold's bum! He was sounding like his dad.

'Oh.' The little one paused to digest what he'd said. 'Will you tell Uncle Merv thank you?'

'Yep, I will.'

'Good. Gotta go. Mum'll be right back, I'm sure,' she

said. 'Nice meeting you!' she added and skipped out of the room.

The little Swamp Thing's mother finished pretending to be a Grongle with the policemen outside. The officer tipped his hat to her and returned to his vehicle. The Pan went back to the sofa and sat down again as the front door banged and she reappeared.

'Hi, I gave Jackie her card,' The Pan said. 'She's a sweet kid.'

She smiled another one of her wonderful smiles but The Pan was less taken in. Having initially had trouble seeing how a creature as hard and uncompromising as Big Merv had managed to hook up with such a gentle and serene, not to mention beautiful, female, he now felt they were as double-hard as one another and made an exceptionally ruthless team.

'The officer said that there had been two reports from people who saw the gentleman he arrested. But one of the descriptions was slightly different.'

Slightly? The Pan wondered.

'He said he would up patrols along the street to make sure we were all safe, just in case it was actually two different beings.'

The Pan raised an eyebrow. 'How very thoughtful of him,' he said.

'It was, wasn't it?' She anticipated his next question. 'We have a back gate onto the next street over. When you leave I expect you would prefer to use that?'

'Thanks.'

'Follow me.'

She led him through the house, past the room full of Jackie and her screaming friends, then through a kitchen to the back door where he stopped to put on his hat and cloak. The garden was huge and mostly grass, with play equipment here and there, a trampoline, swings, a slide. He followed her across the vast lawn to a fence the other side where she unlocked a gate.

'Here, you'd better take some of this with you, too. Jackie would be disappointed if she thought I'd sent you away empty-handed.' She pressed something soft, wrapped in paper napkins, into his palm.

'What is it?' he asked.

'Birthday cake.' She seemed surprised he was even asking.

'Sorry, I should have guessed.' He made to go and then stopped. He took a deep breath. 'Mrs Myrtle.'

'Ms Myrtle,' she corrected him.

'Ms. Sorry. You know, maybe just this once, you should let Jackie buy some non-educational books with her Uncle Merv's present.'

She arched her eyebrows and gave him a bit of a look. 'You think that's a good idea?'

'Yes, I do.' A beat. 'She says she loves stories. If it has to be educational and you can find something fun, I guess she might like a history book.'

'History doesn't have a very happy ending if where we are now is anything to go by.'

'Fair point,' The Pan conceded with a shrug, 'you have me there.'

'It's a good idea though. Stories … I'll think about it,' she said and flashed him another smile. 'See you around.' The gate closed and he was alone on the street.

Chapter 7
Stay or go?

As The Pan started to walk away from the recipients of his first message, he had a strong sense of being completely in over his head. The job had been done but it had gone badly, and whatever Ms Myrtle said, The Pan doubted the security forces would let the broken-nosed bloke go. Yeh and he'd have friends who'd come looking for him, which would start a gang war and Big Merv would tell The Pan it was his fault and kill him.

'Arnold's Y-fronts!' he muttered as he walked.

There was only one thing for it. He'd have to leave Ning Dang Po. As soon as he got his wheels back he'd disappear. Except where would he go? He doubted Glardy or any of the other big cities would be any different and he knew vast areas of Ning Dang Po like the back of his hand. Escape in this city was often as much due to this accrued knowledge as instinct or skill. In a new place it would be skill alone—he'd have to find maps, he'd have to learn the streets. He'd been a GBI for almost three years and compared to anyone else, that was a big number. And the bigger that number got, the bigger the reward on his head and the harder the security forces would try if the opportunity arose to catch him. The Pan wasn't sure he would survive if he started again in a new city he didn't know.

He could go back to Hamgee he supposed. No, he couldn't go back to Hamgee.

Anyway, any other city would have its own organised criminal fraternity, its own versions of Big Merv.

Yep, I may as well stay here and stick with the crap I'm used to, The Pan thought, dourly. He realised he'd slowed up. This wasn't the time to think—this was the time to walk briskly and calmly from the scene of the crime, like a law-abiding citizen going about his business who just happened to be in a bit of a hurry.

Someone had tried to stop him making the drop, even though it was nothing more than a kid's birthday card. Presumably that was usual. There was going to be a reason why Merv's organisation needed runners like The Pan in the first place. Post tampering was clearly it—and not just the kind Government forces would do on Big Merv's real mail if he tried to send his messages through the postal service.

Yep, and there's postman tampering on top, thought The Pan.

Then there was the seemingly graceful, gentle and lovely but clearly totally ruthless Ms Myrtle.

'I was just making a phone call,' she'd said when he arrived. Obviously she was reporting the other bloke. And then afterwards, the way she'd discussed it, as if The Pan and his broken-nosed pursuer were nothing more than commodities to be managed. Yeh, well, they did call employees 'resources' in larger companies. Her attitude probably wasn't so extraordinary. The Pan wondered if he'd been given the job so she could get a look at him, give Big Merv her verdict? Possibly.

What she would say? No way of telling.

Now what, then?

The Pan didn't know so he kept walking towards the end of the street, where he knew there was a main road. Once there, he turned from the quiet backwaters of The Planes onto the busy pavement with relief. He was still twitchy but he was beginning to feel that he'd genuinely escaped this time. With half an eye for signs of danger around him, he moved with the throng of pedestrians, staying on the fringes of large groups where he wouldn't be noticed by the groups themselves, but would be difficult to pick out if anyone was looking for him.

Tonight was going to be grim. He had nowhere to sleep because his wheels were at the mechanic's being repaired and there'd be no guesthouse either because he'd paid for the repairs up front. He opened his wallet and checked his slender resources. No. Not much in there, certainly not enough for a room anywhere.

Gerry the trainee mechanic who looked after The Pan's wheels had promised the work wouldn't be more than forty-eight hours. He'd even offered The Pan his sofa if he needed anywhere to stay nearby. But having a GBI to stay might endanger Gerry's prospects, not to mention his life. He clearly didn't realise that The Pan was blacklisted, but his ignorance wouldn't be considered a defence if the security forces caught him playing host to a GBI. Nope, The Pan was going to have to grit his teeth and spend those two nights on the streets. He'd done it before—the trick was to avoid any contact with the security forces, keep walking, look as if you were busy going somewhere until morning and then sleep during the day.

Arnold's sandals, it was cold though.

It would be, just my luck, The Pan thought to himself.

'Smecking sod and his stupid law,' he muttered. Still, he supposed it could be worse. At least it wasn't snowing.

Chapter 8
Aftermath

The Pan had only been walking twenty minutes and already wished he was somewhere warm. His thoughts turned to The Parrot and Screwdriver, where he'd met Frank and Harry the previous night, and a sudden bolt of inspiration hit him.

'Of course! The pub!' he said aloud. He didn't have to walk *all* night. He could go to The Parrot and Screwdriver and have a drink … 'Although, hang on.'

He stopped and checked his surroundings before getting out his wallet and examining the contents.

'OK, a very small drink.'

Still, that was better than nothing. He could sit and nurse it all night. Now he had a plan, excellent. He was even walking in the right direction. The street he was on, Gauldon Road, lead to Dumpty Street and that led to Market Square, and Turnadot Street led off Market Square too—in fact it was the next street up from Dumpty Street. He stepped out with new purpose.

After such a fear-filled afternoon, The Pan was dog tired. He reflected that in two days' time, as soon as he got the SE2 back, he was going to drive somewhere quiet and have the most massive, gargantuan kip in the history of sleep. But that was two days away. Tonight, after he'd been to the pub, and tomorrow night, he'd be walking. He wrapped his cloak around him and bent his head down against the wind, angling his hat so the blasts of icy air pressed it further onto his head, rather than whipping it off and blowing it away. He walked on for another twenty minutes and realised that his mind was

49

on the wind trajectory over his hat and not on his surroundings. His vigilance was slipping. There were still rush hour commuters on the pavement but they were thinning, and he needed to concentrate on the beings around him, especially any who might be out to get him. A female Galorsh with a pushchair came out of nowhere and rammed into him.

'I'm so sorry,' said The Pan, politely apologising for her lack of awareness.

The shopping bag in the carrier underneath the pushchair split and spilled its load of tangerines all over the pavement. The Pan scrabbled to pick them up for her before the crowds of passing feet damaged them or kicked them away. As he ran to retrieve the last one, which was rolling towards the kerb, he heard tyres squeal. Suddenly the side of a dark blue shiny snurd filled his vision. It stopped beside him and with remarkable alacrity, the driver got out, opened the back passenger door and motioned for The Pan to get in.

The Pan turned to the Galorsh with the pushchair, tangerine in hand, but she'd gone. Not surprisingly—the vehicle parked next to him was a midnight blue snurd MKII. Everyone knew who owned that: Big Merv. The Pan realised he should probably make like the Galorsh with the pushchair and disappear, but he couldn't help noticing that the driver had something in her hand, something that looked remarkably like a firearm. And it was pointing at him. Suddenly, the busy hurrying figures surrounding him a few moments ago seemed to have disappeared.

'Good evening, sir,' said the driver, waiting patiently while The Pan stood panicking. He knew there was no-one else nearby, having used his useful extra pair of eyes to check the street behind him without turning his head, but he still pressed his fingers to his chest and said, 'What? Me?'

'You, sir,' said the driver politely.

The Pan sighed. He'd not thought about this thoroughly enough, of course. Big Merv was bound to want a debrief.

'Me? In there? Only that's a smart set of wheels and I'm—'

'Not smart, sir. No. Mister Merv appreciates that, but he would rather like to talk to you.'

'Mister Merv.' The Pan's heart sank. 'He's in there?'

'No, sir, he is elsewhere, but he asked me to collect you.'

'Smeck.'

The driver nodded to the tangerine in The Pan's hand. 'I'd keep that if I were you. You never know when you'll need a snack.'

'Um ... OK,' squeaked The Pan, fumbling it into his pocket.

The driver was a Blaggysomp, one of the species of K'Barthan from the mountainous region at the centre. She, because this particular Blaggysomp was a lady, had a blue human-like face and was wearing a smart dark suit and a peaked cap. But underneath, The Pan knew, she was covered from head to toe in warm blue fur. Lucky her. She had light brown eyes and though her features were roughly human—well ... setting apart their blueness, of course—they were a little less readable. Even so, The Pan suspected that this was not an offer he should refuse.

'I'm afraid that if you try to run away he's given me full permission to shoot you in the leg. I'd rather not, though, if it's all the same to you.' The driver gestured to the opened door and raised her eyebrows.

Definitely not an offer The Pan could refuse then. He

still thought about running for a moment though, before he did as he was told.

'Right,' said The Pan, 'Yeh, thank you,' and got in.

The door slammed shut and The Pan sank into the luxuriantly upholstered leather seat.

'Put your seatbelt on, lad,' said the driver as the front door slammed.

'Right ...' said The Pan again.

He buckled up and then the chauffeur, or should he call her a chauffeur-ess (The Pan didn't know), was guiding the snurd smoothly into a gap in the traffic. To The Pan's dismay, the doors locked automatically as the vehicle started to move. All was quiet for a moment and then she said, 'It's only a short trip. We're going to the quay.'

Arnold in heaven, the quay. 'Nobody mentioned boxes or cement did they?' whimpered The Pan.

'Eh? No. We're going to The Big Thing, Big Merv's club.'

'We're going clubbing?' asked The Pan incredulously.

'No, well, I'm not, I have to get spruced up and work behind the bar. You might after you've had a word with the boss. His offices are above the club, see?'

'Oh ... right.'

'Yep, it's a quick ten-minute flip.'

The driver seemed approachable and kindly compared to the other members of Big Merv's organisation The Pan had encountered so far. Then again, he was usually either running away from them having nicked something, or, in the case of Frank and Harry, meeting them in the pub after having nicked their boss's wallet. So perhaps it wasn't such a surprise that they'd been angry or hostile. And while the driver had been polite, in other respects she was no different. After all, she had threatened The Pan with a gun. Maybe she just seemed more approachable because she was female.

'Are you … well … you know, the word was that Big Merv used to rob banks … did you ever, you know …?'

'Drive? No,' she laughed, 'that was Hal. He's with the Resistance now, all the drivers are. I'm Bob.'

'Bob? But you're a lady,' said The Pan, blurting out his thoughts before he could stop himself.

'It's short for Roberta. Like I said, I work behind the bar at The Big Thing but I act as Big Merv's chauffeur when he doesn't want to drive the snurd himself.'

'Oh.'

They were turning off the main road now and followed a side street down to a wide open area on the quay. At one end was an old fish-packing plant, now repurposed and repainted, and bedecked with a flashing neon sign proclaiming it 'The Big Thing', a heavily unsubtle pun on Big Merv's nickname.

Bob drove the snurd past a lengthy queue of beings of all shapes and sizes waiting to get in. They had to wait while a Grongolian staff snurd stopped at the front of the queue and disgorged its contents of five officers, who swaggered inside past the peanut-headed bouncers without so much as a glance at the queue of K'Barthans.

'Mister Merv is a respectable businessman,' said Bob. 'A lot of high-echelon Grongles come here to relax. We have the best smoothie menu and the hottest dancers in town.'

'That's nice,' said The Pan weakly. 'Do the Grongles like hot dancers, with all their talk of clean living and that?'

'Do they ever! They're that repressed they're as randy as hell when they think no-one's watching. They mostly go for the human females or the Swamp Things. Us Blaggysomps get less trouble but I still get my bum pinched.'

'I'm sorry to hear that,' said The Pan.

'Oh it's alright, you wouldn't believe how hard you can thump someone and still make it look like an accident.'

The staff snurd pulled away leaving room for Bob to drive Big Merv's MKII past the main entrance to the club and down an access road to the delivery area at the back of the building.

'Here we are.'

To The Pan's dismay, Frank and Harry were waiting to meet him.

'Big Merv is a hard taskmaster but I can tell you for nothing, he's fair,' said Bob as she pressed the button to kill the engine. 'You'll be alright love,' she added and got out.

'I dunno about that,' muttered The Pan in the stillness of the empty snurd. Then Bob was opening the back door and The Pan stepped out onto the concrete.

'About time,. What were you doin', a sightseein' tour?'

'The young gentleman took a little more finding than I expected,' said Bob. 'He's a fast walker.'

She didn't seem unduly bothered by Frank's tone. The Pan, on the other hand, felt what little courage he had rapidly deserting him. He was aware of the usual perspiration starting around his temples as he stumbled nervously to the doorway. Frank pushed him inside.

They stood in a small hallway lit with red lights. The walls and ceiling were red and so was the carpet. There were five doors, including the fire exit through which The Pan had just entered, and a flight of stairs. From behind the furthest door, at the end, came the insistent throbbing beat of music. It reminded The Pan of a heart beat and with the red it made him feel as if he was stuck in some giant sea monster's stomach. He glanced at Frank standing waiting beside him while Harry shut the fire exit. Yeh, one with added gangster-shaped pirates.

As the fire door closed, one of the other doors burst open and a gaggle of three scantily clad human females spilled out of what The Pan realised was the ladies' lavatory.

'Hello Harry,' said one of them, batting her eyelids at the heavy in question.

'Alright sugar.' Harry gave her a brief nod of greeting.

'Catch you later,' she said and the three of them went, giggling, through a second door. The loudness of the music quadrupled for a moment and then abated again as the door banged closed.

'Upstairs,' growled Frank, giving The Pan another shove.

****

Upstairs was a surprisingly utilitarian office. The Pan wasn't sure what he'd expected Big Merv's office to look like, but it wasn't this. There was no ostentatiously applied gold leaf, red velvet plush or similar. Just a functional slatted blind covering the windows, some understated but expensive looking shelving and a battered old roll-top desk with a wooden chair in front of it. The other side of the desk, in a low backed leather swivel chair like the ones The Pan had seen used in newspaper offices in a certain type of film, sat Big Merv. To his right, and The Pan's left, in front of the desk, stood the broken-nosed gentleman who'd been waiting in the phone box at the end of Tallidor Street. The Pan was relieved to see him alive and well but at the same time, as the being who'd been partly responsible for his arrest, The Pan had some misgivings about meeting him now. He hoped he wasn't looking too scared. Hiding his own emotional reaction to things wasn't The Pan's strong suit, but he had a go anyway.

Frank and Harry pushed The Pan forwards and sat him in the chair in front of the desk. They stationed themselves either side of him, each with a hand on one of The Pan's shoulders. There was pressure in those hands and when The Pan tested it, by making to get up again, he felt it increase. Clearly they were there to ensure he remained seated.

Wonderful.

He glanced up at the gentleman from the phone box.

'I'm glad the Grongles released you,' said The Pan, choosing his words carefully because, while it was the truth, 'I'm pleased you're here,' would definitely have been a lie.

The fellow narrowed his eyes and The Pan saw the muscles in his jaw clench. Clearly he was not a happy bunny. The Pan couldn't blame him.

'Shut it!' said Big Merv.

'Sorry,' squeaked The Pan. He turned his attention back to Big Merv.

The trick when negotiating with a Swamp Thing like Big Merv was to keep an eye on what their antennae were doing; if the antennae were moving it meant thought, if they were rigid and sticking straight up in the air it meant the Swamp Thing was angry. Big Merv's were somewhere between the two, moving but kind of stiffly. The Pan chalked it up as his being extremely annoyed and decided to proceed with caution.

Without further preamble, Big Merv cut to the chase. 'I wanna know what you done today.'

In his panic The Pan took him literally. 'I nicked a

plate of eggs Benedict for breakfast from Sam's Brasserie in the covered market then I—'

'Don't push it, son,' said Big Merv wearily, although to The Pan's relief, his antennae seemed to relax a bit. 'I'm talking about the drop you done and you know it.'

The Pan didn't but decided it was best not to admit it. 'It … went OK.'

The heavy who'd been waiting for The Pan took an angry breath in. But instead of speaking, he folded his arms. This was standard thug policy to make the biceps look bigger and the thug scarier. It worked. The Pan could feel more cold sweat forming on his temples and pricking at his palms.

Big Merv nodded towards the guy standing by the desk and said, 'That ain't what Fists says.'

Arnold, no. The Pan tried to look calm and in control but it was very difficult when he was shaking the way a particularly wobbly jelly might if it was being wheeled over some bumpy cobbles in a sack barrow.

The pressure on The Pan's shoulders from Frank and Harry increased. Arnold's bottom! What on earth had 'Fists' said? There was no way of knowing. The Pan was keen to save himself a beating, or worse, but preferably without alienating Fists. Whatever the fellow had told Big Merv, The Pan's story had to line up with it.

'I was a little early,' he squeaked playing for time.

'An' Fists followed you?'

'No, he—'

'Don't lie to me, you little smeck.'

The Pan took a deep breath, aware that contradicting someone twice his size, who clearly wanted an excuse to thump him, or at least an excuse to let someone else do it, went strongly against his personal health and safety protocol. But in this instance, it was better than the alternative which might, possibly, involve becoming a motorway stanchion.

'I wasn't followed, he was waiting for me. Right?'

Fist's eyes narrowed a tiny bit more but he said nothing.

Arnold's snot! Was that a yes? A no? Or what? Had the guy told Big Merv a different story? What to say? It would be extremely stupid to offend a bloke this big and ferocious-looking by getting him a telling off from the boss, for example. The Pan had enough on his plate with the Grongles—he didn't any need more large psychotic beings out to get him than necessary.

'Give me a hand here, did you follow me without my noticing?' asked The Pan, knowing it was impossible.

'Fists ain't gonna be sayin' nothing,' said Big Merv.

'Right.' The Pan took another deep breath to try and steady his nerves and more importantly, his voice. Calm was all-important in a situation like this. He took a moment to collect himself, looking down at his shaking hands and trying to gather his thoughts, but they seemed to have made a run for it. 'OK. First I saw of Mister Fists was when he waited for me in the phone box,' said The Pan.

'We're listenin'.'

Arnold's armpits! Keep calm, show no fear. 'I reckoned he knew I was coming and was waiting there for me—my apologies if I've got that wrong Mister Fists, sir—'

'You ain't talkin' to Fists, you're talking to me,' growled Big Merv.

'Sorry.' The Pan cleared his throat. He was feeling a bit sick, fear of course. Even so, he hoped he wasn't going to hurl. 'When I saw Mr Fists, I thought he looked like an enforcer. In fact I thought he might be one of your enforcers and that this was a test until your friend Ms Myrtle dobbed him in and the security forces carted him off.'

'How d'you know she dobbed him in?' asked Big Merv and The Pan couldn't help noticing that his voice had acquired a sinister edge.

'She took a while to let me in.' Just the thought of those moments standing at the gate, as Fists and the police closed in, made The Pan's blood run cold. 'She apologised for taking her time and said she was making a call.'

'Yer. Checks out,' said Big Merv. The leather seat creaked as he leaned suddenly forward towards The Pan. 'That leaves me with a conundrum.'

'It does?'

'Yer. See, some of my lads reckon you're bad news.'

'Right,' said The Pan.

'Yer, an' you were bad news for Fists, 'ere, that's for deffo.'

'I'm really sorry Mister F—' began The Pan and Big Merv spoke calmly over him.

'Shut it, pipsqueak. Luckily for Fists, I got lawyers.'

'Sorry, but—'

'I said shut it!' bellowed Big Merv. The Pan managed to stifle a scream but couldn't help letting out a small whimper. 'I was outa town last night an' I left the boys in charge.' The world's only orange Swamp Thing shrugged open the leather trench coat he was wearing and reached into the inside pocket of his immaculate pinstriped suit. The Pan felt the hairs on the back of his neck stand up. He wanted to run but Frank and Harry anticipated it and the pressure on his shoulders increased. He wouldn't be able to wriggle free, not at the moment anyway, so he stared at Big Merv, trying not to show the turmoil inside him and praying that The Big

Thing wasn't going to pull a gun on him. Few things scared The Pan more than guns, especially when he found himself at the wrong end of one.

What if Big Merv shot him?

No, he wouldn't do that here. It would mess up the carpet. If The Pan was going to be killed surely they'd all be at the Outer Ring Road or beside the river somewhere, not here. Calm, breathe … Big Merv took out a folded paper with a flourish.

'Like I said, while I was outa town, the boys found this.'

He held it up.

'Right,' said The Pan as he stared at the wanted poster with his name on it.

'Nice picture, innit?' Big Merv's tone was almost conversational but his antennae weren't moving at all. He was angry. 'They ain't got yer nose right though. An' if they wanted anyone to recognise you, they shoulda done one with yer hat on.'

'Right.'

'Yer, "right". Fists, show this to the little squirt so he can have a proper look.'

Fists took the paper, leaned down intimidatingly close and held it in front of The Pan's face. Unfortunately, he got a bit enthusiastic with the whole business of being scary and the poster was too close to read. But since The Pan had already read it while Big Merv was holding it up, he decided not to say anything. To his relief, there was no mention of him being on the blacklist.

'When Frank an' Harry saw this,' Big Merv pointed at the poster Fists was holding, 'they reckoned I shoulda slotted yer.'

The Pan swallowed. His throat had gone dry.

'Right,' he croaked.

'An' what's more, they reckoned that if I'd known about this, that I woulda done. So they sent Fists down the drop-off.'

'To kill me?'

'Nah, you great spanner! No-one gets killed in this organisation unless I say so. He went to get the package an' do the delivery.'

'Right.'

'Listen you little runt, if you say "right" one more time I'm gonna be forced to ask Fists 'ere to punch you.'

'Riiiii … OK,' The Pan hurriedly corrected himself as Big Merv's eyes narrowed. The Pan checked his boss's antennae again. They were still standing straight up in a sure sign of annoyance. There was a brief hiatus while Fists handed back the poster.

'"The Pan of Hamgee",' Big Merv read aloud. 'So it is your real name.' The Pan shrugged. It was his father's title and since his father and his older brother, the rightful recipient, were both dead, he'd made it his. No-one knew his birth name these days and he was happy to keep it that way. ''S a fair way away innit, Hamgee?'

'Yeh.'

'Yer. I'm guessin' you don't want these folks what put this poster up knowing you is 'ere?'

'No, sir.'

''S right. An' I reckon that means you ain't gonna cause me no bother because I reckon you like bein' alive.'

'Yes,' said The Pan, with more feeling than he'd intended, because he did like being alive even on the blacklist, even now. Sure, being alive at this actual, precise moment wasn't pleasant; trapped in a confined space with some scary gangsters in a state of utter terror, but it was still better than being dead. Probably.

''S right. I reckon you do. So what're you gonna do?'

'Stay off your patch?' The Pan's voice came out a bit higher and more squeaky than he'd intended.

'Nah, you big skipping rope,' Big Merv laughed with absolutely zero humour. 'You don't get away that easy. You're mine now, mate. Geddit?'

'Um, ri— Yeh, I get it.'

'Sweet. Ms Myrtle reckons you done good today. Reckoned it was Fists or you. She knows Fists and she knows I got lawyers so it was Fists coz she don't know you. Now I seen this,' the paper crackled as he waved the poster again, 'I ain't so sure any lawyer on the planet's gonna get you outa the crap you've got yourself into. Once you gotta record, son, it sticks.'

'Yes,' The Pan's voice sounded more trembly than he wanted it to. 'That's probably true. Look, Big Merv ...' there was a palpable increase in tension in the room,

'... sorry Big Merv, sir,' the tension subsided a fraction, 'I'll be honest. I have ... fiscal difficulties. That's why I steal sometimes, because I have to.'

Big Merv put his hand into his jacket pocket, but on the other side this time. Even though he knew Big Merv was unlikely to kill someone indoors, let alone in his own office, The Pan still couldn't stop himself from cowering back in the seat and raising his arms in front of his face.

'What in Arnold's name are you doin', you little nerk?' demanded Big Merv in what appeared to be genuine amazement. When The Pan tried to straighten up in his seat, Frank and Harry eased the pressure on his shoulders a bit so he could which was uncharacteristically accommodating of them.

'I thought you had a gun,' The Pan explained sheepishly as Big Merv pulled out his wallet. By The Prophet this was embarrassing, now, as well as scary.

The Pan could feel his face burning up in a deep, dark blush.

The Big Thing was looking at him with an incredulous expression. 'I'm a businessman, why would I be packin'? Arnold's trousers! You don't half scare easy,' he chuckled.

'You're not wrong there,' said The Pan. 'That's why Frank and Harry are right, I'd be a rubbish delivery man.'

'Nah,' Big Merv shook his head and pointed his finger at The Pan for emphasis as he added, 'I reckon that makes you proper handy; better than anyone.'

'I'm not sure I'll be—'

'You ain't got no option, pal. You made your choice when you nicked my wallet. You took my cash an' you done the job. You done it your way but you still done it an' you done it good enough. That means ...' he opened the wallet one handed and flicked out a couple of notes, holding them up between his fingers, then transferred them to his other hand and held them out '... you get paid.'

Fists stepped forward, took the notes from Big Merv's hand and as The Pan sat in the chair, shaking with fear, still held by Frank and Harry, the bruiser leaned down and stuffed them into The Pan's jacket pocket.

'Thanks.'

Fists nodded and flashed him a snarling sinister smile that scared The Pan so much that he was afraid he might faint.

'Thing is, son,' Big Merv lectured, 'I know a bloke what I can use when I see one, and you're it. So I'm gonna give you more deliveries to do, an' you're gonna make 'em. You got that?'

'Yes, Big Merv, sir,' whispered The Pan.

Big Merv's leather trench coat creaked as he put his wallet back in his inside pocket, folded his arms and glared at The Pan in silence. His felt-tip green eyes met The Pan's blue ones and, for all his efforts to hold his head up high and maintain eye contact, The Pan looked away first.

Big Merv sat for a moment, seemingly relaxed and content, his antennae moving backwards and forward as he thought. He unfolded his arms and drummed his fingers on the desk. The Pan watched and waited, his emotions fluctuating from terror, to hope, to confusion and everything in between. It appeared that business between them was concluded, except for the small matter of his being released.

Eventually the tension was too much and he spoke.

'Mr Big Merv, sir,' he cringed, 'um ... can I go now? Please.' He couldn't help noticing that his words were getting fainter and fainter as the sentence progressed until he hardly did more than mouth the 'please' at the end.

'In a mo,' said Big Merv, but he nodded at Frank and Harry who released their grip on The Pan's shoulders.

'Ri—' began The Pan. Big Merv rose abruptly to his feet and Fists stepped forwards, arm pulled back ready to throw a punch. The Pan swallowed. 'Sorry, I meant alright, anything you say, sir, boss, sir,' he gabbled.

''S better. There ain't gonna be no more misunderstandings with the boys,' said Big Merv, perhaps as much for Frank, Harry and Fists's benefit as for The Pan's. You might get some flack but it won't be nothing major. I've had a word before you turned up an' I've told 'em to play nice. Right boys?'

'Yer,' the three of them agreed sullenly.

Arnold's socks! If Big Merv really had 'had a word' as he put it, The Pan knew he'd get a lot more than flack. He bit back his instinctive reply which was to ask Big Merv if this was simply a very ornate way to kill him.

'That means you gotta play nice an' all.'

'Thank you.' The Pan took all his courage and said, 'Thank you Frank, Harry and Fists for your understanding. I will.'

'Pukka.' Big Merv clapped his hands and rubbed them together, making The Pan jump. 'Alright lads, off you go,' and as The Pan stood to follow Frank, Harry and Fists out of the room Big Merv added, 'Not you.'

By The Prophet's bogies!

The Pan waited and Big Merv came round the desk and stood in front of him. Arnold's trollies! He was definitely a very large being, even for a Swamp Thing. It felt as if he was blocking out the light.

'Listen, son. Them blokes are 'ard men. You gotta earn their respect. Do that an' they'll accept you.'

Great. No pressure. Suddenly, The Pan felt as if he was being lectured by his dad all over again. 'I'll try.'

'Sweet,' said Big Merv, who clearly considered the matter closed. 'I know it ain't easy but they'll appreciate the effort.'

'I'll remember that,' said The Pan weakly.

'Good. You can remember something else an' all. You know that pub where you met Frank an' Harry?'

'The Parrot and Screwdriver?'

'Yer, that's the one. Harry an' Frank didn't like it down there. Said they served 'em dodgy beer.'

'Yes,' said The Pan, 'I got that impression.'

'Yer but they reckoned your beer looked alright. They reckoned you were a hit.'

The Pan made a mental note that Frank and Harry were clearly a great deal more capable at picking up nuance and small details than they made out. 'I seemed to get on OK.'

'Yer,' Big Merv nodded. 'I reckon. You gonna go there again?'

The Pan thought about it. Should he lie? No, he may as well be honest. 'Yes, I think so.'

'Regular?'

The Pan remembered the beer and sandwiches he'd had, the way the old ladies and Their Trev had made him feel welcome. He thought how The Parrot and Screwdriver was the only place he'd been to since being blacklisted where he'd felt at home.

'Yes.'

'Sweet. Then this is how it's gonna go down. When you wanna be out of the way, no-one's gonna bother you there. But at the same time see, we're gonna know where you are. An' if I wanna job done, you're gonna get a letter care of them little old dears what runs that pub.'

'There is a chance they'll change their minds about me and throw me out.'

'Yer but I reckon they ain't gonna do that, son.'

'You do?'

'Yer. I trust Frank an' Harry an' I reckon they've got that set-up bang to rights. You're well in. I'll tell you something else an' all. You're gonna get a good feel for this city drinkin' in there.'

'I am?'

'Yer. 'S a lotta interesting blokes an' ladies what drinks down that pub.'

'There are?'

'Yer an' you're gonna get to know 'em.'

'I am?'

'Yer. 'S complicated, being the boss, but if you wanna stay on top then sometimes, to keep things running smoothly, there have to be places where folks know you don't go. Course, if you got a bloke there listening out for anything interesting you get to hear what other blokes are saying; the kind of blokes what go there because you don't, an' you get to know stuff they don't want you to know, an' that brings results. You get me?'

'Are you asking me to spy on the punters?' asked The Pan.

'Nah, you giant tool bit! You ain't gonna grass up no-one. I mean listen out. Like I said, Frank an' Harry reckon you're trouble, with a capital T. They ain't wrong, pal, I *know* you're trouble, but I reckon you're trouble I can use. Coz you're smart, an' all.

'The lads think I shoulda chucked you in the river. They may have a point, but I've told 'em it ain't gonna happen yet. An' what that means for you, is that I've generously saved your arse an' you owe me.' Big Merv poked a pointy finger in The Pan's chest as he said the 'you owe me' bit. 'You ain't gonna talk to me again course, unless you make a proper stuff-up. Coz it ain't my job, dealin' with small fry. But when I wanna certain kind of message delivered you'll be hearing from one of the lads; Frank or Harry or someone else, Fists maybe, or one of the lasses like Bob behind the bar. An' on top of that, if I wanna know what a certain group of folks thinks, I'm gonna ask the lads that too, an' they're gonna ask you, and I reckon you're gonna know without needin' to ask no-one coz you drink in that pub. An' for that, I'm gonna pay you a bit here an' there. Not much, but if you do good maybe there'll be more.'

'Thank you.'

'Yer. You listen to 'em good—some of the stuff you hear might keep you alive an' all.' Big Merv handed him two more notes. 'You go down Dancing Sally's on Frontock Street an' tell 'er I sent you. She may give you a room for that,' he said.

'Thank you,' said The Pan again.

'Yer. Now, get outa here. I got stuff to do.'

****

As soon as he reached the bottom of the stairs, The Pan checked the denominations on the notes Big Merv had given him. Not a great deal. Maybe Dancing Sally's was a total dive, or maybe she just wasn't expensive. Or maybe the smart move would be to keep walking tonight the way he'd planned and hold the money in reserve for harder times. As he stepped out into the icy darkness he glanced at his watch and realised it was late, but not so late that he'd miss last orders at The Parrot and Screwdriver if he walked quickly. Yeh and he had enough cash for a half pint of Humbert's Wallsmacker.

Should he?

Yeh. Whatever he decided—Dancing Sally's or a night on the streets—he may as well begin the evening sitting down … with a beer.

And some of those speciality cheese and pickle sandwiches, he thought.

He smiled to himself.

'Yeh,' he said quietly, 'and I have the perfect excuse.' After all, every time he visited that pub from now on, he'd be doing Big Merv a favour. He adjusted his hat, threw the corner of his cloak over his shoulder and strode away into the night.

The end

Other books by M T McGuire

There are more books in this series. If you'd like to find out what happens next, look out for the next book in this series:

Nothing to See Here
K'Barthan Extras, Hamgeean Misfit: No 2

It's midwinter and preparations for the biggest religious festival in the K'Barthan year are in full swing. Yes, even though, officially, religious activity has been banned no-one is going to ignore Arnold, The Prophet's birthday, especially not Big Merv, who orders The Pan of Hamgee to deliver the traditional Prophet's Birthday gift to his accountants and lawyers.

As usual, The Pan has managed to elicit the unwanted attention of the security forces. Can he make the delivery and get back to the Parrot and Screwdriver pub in time for an unofficial Prophet's Birthday celebration with his friends?

You can also read more about The Pan of Hamgee's adventures in K'Barth in a series of four full-length books.

The K'Barthan Series

All The Pan of Hamgee wants is a quiet life.

So why did he have to fall in love with a woman living a different version of reality, upset a murderous tyrant and then run out of places to hide?

Now all he has to do is face his inner demons, rescue everything he holds dear and save the world, or die trying.

Oh yes, and he's an abject coward.

Great. No pressure then.

Escape From B-Movie Hell

Bronze Medal winner, Wishing Shelf Book Award, 2015.

If you asked Andi Turbot whether she had anything in common with Flash Gordon she'd say no, emphatically.

Saving the world is for dynamic, go-ahead leaders of men. And while it would be nice to see a woman getting involved for a change, she believes she could be the least well-equipped being in her galaxy for the job.

Then her best friend Eric reveals that he's an extraterrestrial. He's not just any E.T. either. He's Gamalian: seven feet tall, lobster-shaped and covered in marmite-scented goo. Just when Andi's getting used to that he tells her about the apocalypse and really ruins her day.

The human race will perish unless Eric's Gamalian superiors step in. Abducted and trapped on an alien ship, Andi must convince the Gamalians her world is worth saving. Or escape from their clutches and save it herself.

For more information vist: www.hamgee.co.uk/books

Author News

Never miss a new release again! Sign up for M T Mail. Just visit this link: http://www.hamgee.co.uk/freebook

You can choose to hear about everything or just new releases. You can also keep up to date with all things K'Barthan and M T McGuire by joining her K'Barthan Jolly Japery Facebook Group.

To join, go here: http://bit.ly/JollyJapes

Or you can follow M T McGuire on these social media:

Website: http://www.hamgee.co.uk
Blog: http://www.mtmcguire.co.uk
Instagram: @mtmcguire
Twitter: @mtmcguireauthor

BV - #0116 - 250923 - C0 - 203/133/5 - PB - 9781907809309 - Matt Lamination